John Ruskin

Dilecta

Correspondence, diary notes, and extracts from books, illustrating

Praeterita

John Ruskin

Dilecta

Correspondence, diary notes, and extracts from books, illustrating Praeterita

ISBN/EAN: 9783337019648

Printed in Europe, USA, Canada, Australia, Japan

Cover: Foto ©Andreas Hilbeck / pixelio.de

More available books at **www.hansebooks.com**

DILECTA.

CORRESPONDENCE, DIARY NOTES, AND

EXTRACTS FROM BOOKS,

ILLUSTRATING

PRÆTERITA.

ARRANGED BY

JOHN RUSKIN, LL.D.,

HONORARY STUDENT OF CHRIST CHURCH,
AND HONORARY FELLOW OF CORPUS CHRISTI COLLEGE, OXFORD.

PART I.

GEORGE ALLEN,
SUNNYSIDE, ORPINGTON, KENT.
1886.

Printed by Hazell, Watson, & Viney, Ld., London and Aylesbury.

PREFACE.

THE readers of PRÆTERITA must by this time have seen that the limits of its design do not allow the insertion of any but cardinal correspondence. They will, of course, also know that during a life like mine, I must have received many letters of general interest, while those of my best-regarded friends are often much more valuable than my own sayings. Of these I will choose what I think should not be lost, which, with a few excerpts of books referred to, I can arrange at odd times for the illustration of PRÆTERITA, while yet the subscribers to that work need not buy the supplemental one unless they like. But, for the convenience of those who wish to have both, their form and type will be the same.

The letters will not be arranged chrono-
logically, but as they happen, at any time,
to bear on the incidents related in the
main text. Thus I begin with some of
comparatively recent date, from my very
dear friend Robert Leslie, George Leslie's
brother, of extreme importance in illustration of points in the character of Turner
to which I have myself too slightly referred.
The pretty scene first related in them,
however, took place before I had heard
Turner's name. The too brief notes of
autobiography left by the quietly skilful
and modest painter, the " father who was
staying at Lord Egremont's," C. R. Leslie,
contain the truest and best-written sketches
of the leading men of his time that, so far
as I know, exist in domestic literature.

J. RUSKIN.

BRANTWOOD, 26th June, 1886.

DILECTA.

———◆——

"6, MOIRA PLACE, SOUTHAMPTON,

"*June 7th*, 1884.

"My father was staying at Lord Egremont's; it was in September, I believe, of 1832. The sun had set beyond the trees at the end of the little lake in Petworth Park; at the other end of this lake was a solitary man, pacing to and fro, watching five or six lines or trimmers, that floated outside the water lilies near the bank. 'There,' said my father, 'is Mr. Turner, the great *sea** painter.' He was smoking

---

* I have put 'sea' in italics, because it is a new idea to me that at this time Turner's fame rested on his marine paintings — all the early drawings passing virtually without notice from the Art world.

1

a cigar, and on the grass, near him, lay a fine pike. As we came up, another fish had just taken one of the baits, but, by some mischance, this line got foul of a stump or tree root in the water, and Turner was excited and very fussy in his efforts to clear it, knotting together bits of twine, with a large stone at the end, which he threw over the line several times with no effect. 'He did not care,' he said, 'so much about losing the fish as his tackle.' My father hacked off a long slender branch of a tree and tried to poke the line clear. This also failed, and Turner told him that nothing but a boat would enable him to get his line. Now it chanced that, the very day before, Chantrey, the sculptor, had been trolling for jack, rowed about by a man in a boat nearly all day; and my father, thinking it hard that Turner should lose his fish and a valuable line, started across the park to a keeper's cottage, where the key of the boathouse was kept. When we returned, and while waiting for the boat, Turner became quite chatty, rigging me a little ship, cut out of a chip, sticking masts into it, and making her sails from a leaf or two torn from a small sketch-book, in which I recollect seeing a memorandum in colour that he had made of the sky and sunset. The ship was hardly ready for sea before the man and boat came lumbering up to the bank, and Turner was busy directing and helping him to recover the line, and, if possible, the fish. This, however, escaped in the confusion. When the line was got in, my father gave the man a couple of shillings for bringing the boat; while Turner, remarking that it was no use fishing any more after the water had been so much disturbed, reeled up his other lines, and, slipping a finger through the pike's gills, walked off with us toward Petworth House. Walking behind, admiring the great fish, I noticed as Turner carried it how the tail dragged on the grass, while his own coat-tails were but little further from the ground; also that a roll of sketches, which I picked up, fell from a pocket in one of these coat-tails, and Turner, after letting my father have a peep at them, tied the bundle up tightly with a bit of the sacred line. I think he had taken some twine off this bundle of sketches when making his stone rocket apparatus, and that this led to the roll working out of his pocket. My father knew little about fishing or fishing-tackle, and asked Turner, as a matter of curiosity, what the line he had nearly lost was worth. Turner answered that it was an expensive one, worth quite half a crown.

"Turner's fish was served for dinner that evening; and, though I was not there to hear it, my father told me how

old Lord Egremont joked Chantrey much
about his having trolled the whole of the
day without even a single run, while
Turner had only come down by coach
that afternoon, gone out for an hour, and
brought in this big fish. Sir Francis was
a scientific fisherman, and president of the
Stockbridge Fishing Club, and, no doubt,
looked upon Turner, with his trimmers,
as little better than a poacher. Still there
was the fish, and Lord Egremont's banter
of Chantrey must have been an intense
delight to Turner as a fisherman.

"It was about this time that I first
went with my father to the Royal Academy
upon varnishing days, and, wandering about
watching the artists at work, there was no
one, next to Stanfield and his boats, that
I liked to get near so much as Turner,
as he stood working upon those, to my
eyes, nearly blank white canvases in their
old academy frames. There were always
a number of mysterious little gallipots and

cups of colour ranged upon drawing stools
in front of his pictures; and, among other
bright colours, I recollect one that must
have been simple red-lead. He used short
brushes, some of them like the writers
used by house decorators, working with
thin colour over the white ground, and
using the brush end on, dapping and writing
with it those wonderfully fretted cloud
forms and the ripplings and filmy surface
curves upon his near water. I have seen
Turner at work upon many varnishing
days, *but never remember his using a
maul-stick.** He came, they said, with the
carpenters at six in the morning, and
worked standing all day. He always had
on an old, tall beaver hat, worn rather
off his forehead, which added much to
his look of a North Sea pilot.

* Italics mine. I have often told my pupils,
and, I hope, printed for them somewhere, that
all fine painting involves the play, or sweep,
of the arm from the shoulder.

(Parenthetic.) " Have you noticed the sky lately in the north-west when the sun is about a hand's breadth above the horizon; also just after sunset, when your 'storm cloud' has been very marked, remaining like a painted sky, so still, that it might have been photographed over and over again by the slowest of processes?

(From a following letter):—

"The only thing I am not certain about is the exact date of that first sight of Turner. I know that in 1833 I did not go to Petworth, as my father took us all to America in the autumn of that year, returning again in the spring of '34; and I am inclined to think that the scene in the park, which I tried to describe, must have taken place in the September of '34. I remember it all as though it were yesterday; I must then have been eight years old. I was always with my father, and we spent every autumn at Petworth for many years, both before and after then. I did not think it worth mentioning, but I had been allowed to spend the whole of the day before with Sir Francis Chantrey in that boat, and recollect his damning the man very much, once during the day, for pulling ahead rather suddenly, whereby Sir Francis, who was standing up in the boat, was thrown upon his back in the bottom of her—no joke for such a heavy man.

"I think the foundation of *the ship* was a mere flat bit of board or chip, cut out for me by my father, and that Constable, the artist, had stuck a sail in it for me some days before (he was also at Petworth). I must have mentioned this to Turner, as I have a recollection of his saying, as he rigged it, 'Oh, he don't know anything about ships,' or 'What does he know about ships? this is how it ought to be,' sticking up some sails which looked to my eyes really quite ship-shape at that time.

"I saw Turner painting at the R.A. on more than one varnishing day, as my father took me with him for several years in succession. Every academician, in those good old times of *many* varnishing days, was allowed to take an assistant or servant with him, to carry about and clean his brushes, etc.; and my father and others always took their sons. This went on for some years, and I recollect my disappointment when my father told me he could not take me any more, as there had been a resolution passed at a council meeting against the custom. I know that most of the pictures which I saw Turner working upon, just as I have described to you, were the Venetian subjects. Mr. Turner was always rather pleasant and friendly with me, on account, I think, of my love of the sea. I have been to his house in Queen Anne Street

many times with my father, and recollect
once that he took us into his dining-room
and uncorked a very fine old bottle of
port for us. I was much older then,
perhaps fifteen or sixteen. I can never of
course forget a few kind words which he
spoke to me when I was myself an ex-
hibitor at the R.A. My picture was a
scene on the deck of a ship of two sailors
chaffing a passenger, called 'A Sailor's Yarn.'
Turner came up to the picture, and after
looking at it for a minute, said, ' I like
your colour.' I have the picture now, and
always think of him when I look at it.

" I have written all this in great haste
to answer your questions, dear Mr. Ruskin;
and am sorry I have so little to tell, and
that I am obliged to bring myself forward
so much in the matter.

" I have often thought that Turner went
out to catch that pike because he knew that
Chantrey had been unsuccessful the day before.

" I don't know whether you were ever

a fisherman; if you were, you would understand the strange fascination that the water has from which you snatched your first fish, after feeling the tug and sweep of it upon the line. Now the lake in Petworth Park had that fascination for my early fishy mind. Most boys' minds are very fishy, and shooty too,* as you have pointed out, and I was no exception; but I was always intensely boaty as well, caring less for rowing than sailing; and when I could not get afloat myself, I was never tired, even as a big boy, of doing so in imagination in any form of toy sailing-boat I could devise or get hold of. Hence it was that when I saw Turner's fish upon the grass, and was told that he was a sea painter, I looked upon

---

* Dear Leslie, might we not as well say they were bird's-nesty or dog-fighty? Really useful fishing is not play; and to watch a trout is indeed, whether for boy or girl, greater pleasure than to catch it, if they did but know!

him at once as something to fall down
and worship — a man who could catch a
big fish, and paint sea and boats! My
father, though he had much of the back-
woodsman in his nature, and could make
himself a bootjack in five minutes when
he had mislaid or lost his own, was no
sportsman, and cared little for boating
beyond taking a shilling fare sometimes
from Hungerford Stairs in a wherry.

"As to my recollections of Turner upon
the varnishing days, you must bear in mind
that, as I had been used to spend from a
child many hours a day in a painting-
room, I never recollect a time when I
was not well up in all matters relating to
paint and brushes; and the first thing
that struck me about Turner, as he
worked at the R.A., was, that his way of
work was quite unlike that of the other
artists; and it had at once a great interest
for me, so that I believe I watched him
often for long spells at a time. I noticed,

as I think I told you, that his brushes were few, looked old, and that among them were some of those common little soft brushes in white quill used by house-painters for painting letters, etc., with. His colours were mostly in powder, and he mixed them with turpentine, sometimes with size, and water, and perhaps even with stale beer, as the grainers do their umber when using it upon an oil ground, binding it in with varnish afterwards; this way of painting is fairly permanent, as one knows by the work known to them as wainscotting or oak-graining. Besides red-lead, he had a blue which looked very like ordinary smalt; this, I think, tempered with crimson or scarlet lake, he worked over his near waters in the darker lines. I am almost sure that I saw him at work on the *Téméraire*, and that he altered the effect after I first saw it. In fact, I believe he worked again on this picture in his house long after I first saw it in the R.A.

I remember Stanfield at work too, and what a contrast his brushes and whole manner of work presented to that of Turner.

"My brother George tells me to-day that he too has seen Turner at work, once at the R.A., and describes him as seeming to work almost with his nose close to the picture. He says that the picture was that one of the railway engine coming towards us at full speed. But my brother is nearly ten years younger than I am. Turner was always full of little mysterious jokes and fun with his brother artists upon these varnishing days; and my father used to say that Turner looked upon them as one of the greatest privileges of the Academy. It is such a pleasure to me to think that I can be of *any* use to *you*, that I have risked sending this after my other letters. I have always been a man more or less of lost opportunities, and when living some fifteen years ago at Deal one occurred to me that I have never ceased to regret. My next-door neighbour was an old lady of the name of Cato; her maiden name was White; and she told me that she knew Turner well as a young man, also the young lady he was in love with. She spoke of him as being very delicate, and said that he often came to Margate for health. She seemed to know little of Turner as the artist. I cannot tell you how much I regret now not having pushed my inquiries further at that time; but twenty years ago I was more or less an unregenerate ruffian in such matters; and though I have always felt the same for Turner as the artist, I cared little to know much more than I remembered myself of him as a man.

"Trusting you will forgive the haste again of this letter,

"Believe me, dear Mr. Ruskin,

"Yours faithfully,

"ROBT. LESLIE."

"Out of many visits to the house in Queen Anne Street, I never saw or was admitted to Turner's working studio, though he used to pop out of it upon us, in a mysterious way, during our stay in his gallery, and then leave us again for a while. In fact, I think my father had leave to go there when he pleased. I particularly remember one visit, in company with my father and a Yankee sea captain, to whom Turner was very polite, evidently looking up to the sailor capacity, and making many little apologies for the want of ropes and other details about certain vessels in a picture. No one knew or felt, I think, better than Turner the want of these mechanical details, and while the sea captain was there he paid no attention to any one else, but followed him about the gallery, bent upon hearing all he said. As it turned out, this captain and he became good friends, for the Yankee skipper's eyes were sharp enough to see through all the fog and mystery of Turner, how much of real sea feeling there was in him and his work. Captain Morgan, who was a great friend of Dickens, my father, and many other artists, used to send Turner a box of cigars almost every voyage after that visit to Queen Anne Street.

"Nothing I can ever do or write for you would repay the good you have done for me and mine in your books; and will you allow me to say, that in reading them I am not (much as I admire it) carried actually off my legs by your style, but that I feel more and more, each day I live, the plain *practical truth* of *all* you tell us. I cannot bear to hear people talk and write as they do of your style, and your being the greatest master of it, etc, while they sneer at the matter, etc. Nothing lowers the present generation of what are called clever men more to me than this" (nay, is not their abuse of Carlyle's manner worse than their praise of mine?). "I am rather thankful, even, that my best friends here do not belong to this class, being mostly pilots, sea captains, boat-builders, fishermen, and the like.

"I shall, in a day or two, be with my mother at Henley-on-Thames, and if I learn anything more from her about Turner, will let you know. She is now eighty-four, but writes a better letter, in a finer hand, without glasses, than I can with them.

"6, MOIRA PLACE, SOUTHAMPTON,
"*June 25th*, 1884.

"DEAR MR. RUSKIN,

"I have before me the engraving by Wilmore of the *Téméraire*. I think it was Stanfield who told me that the rigging of the ship in this engraving was trimmed up and generally made intelligible to the engraver by some mechanical marine artist or other. I am not sure now who, but think it was Duncan; whether or no, the rigging is certainly not as Turner painted

it; while the black funnel of the tug
in the engraving is placed abaft her mast
or flagpole, instead of before it, as in
Turner's picture; his first, strong, almost
prophetic idea of smoke, soot, iron, and
steam, coming to the front in all naval
matters, being thus changed and, I venture
to think, weakened by this alteration.
You most truly told us years ago that
' Take it all in all, a ship of the line is
the most honourable thing that man, as
a gregarious animal, has ever produced.'
I shall not therefore hesitate to ask you
to put on your best spectacles and look
for a moment at the enclosed photograph,
which I have had taken for you from
a model of the *Téméraire*, which we
have here now in a sort of museum.
The model is nearly three feet long, and
belonged to an old naval man; it was
made years ago by the French prisoners
in the hulks at Portsmouth out of their
beef-bones! Even if we were at war with

France, and had the men and ships likely
to do it, it would be impossible to catch
any prisoners now who could make such
a ship as this out of anything, much
less of beef-bones; and as I foresee that
this lovely little ship must soon, in the
nature of things, pass away (some unfeeling
brute has already robbed her of all her
boats), and that there will be no one living
able to restore a rope or spar rightly
once they are broken or displaced in her,
I felt it almost a duty to have this record
taken and to send you a copy of it. I
focussed the camera myself, but there is,
unavoidably, some exaggeration of the
length of her jibboom and flying-jibboom.
These spars, however, in old ships really
measured, together with the bowsprit,
nearly the length of the foremast from
deck to truck. In fact, the bowsprit, with
its spritsail and spritsail-topsailyards, formed
a sort of fourth mast.

" I have just returned from a visit to

my dear old mother at Henley, and she told me of how Turner came up to our house one evening by special appointment to sup upon Welsh rabbit (toasted cheese). This must have been about the year 1840 or '41, as it was at the time my father was engaged upon a portrait of Lord Chancellor Cottenham; and during the evening Turner went into the painting-room, where the robes, wig, etc., of the Chancellor were arranged upon a lay-figure; and, after a little joking, he was persuaded to put on the Lord Chancellor's wig, in which, my mother says, Turner looked splendid, so joyous and happy, too, in the idea that the Chancellor's wig became him better than any one else of the party.

"I must have been away from home then, I think in America, for I never should have forgotten Turner being at our house; and this, I believe, is the only time he ever was there.

"Turner, my father, and the Yankee captain were excellent friends about this time, as the captain took a picture of Turner's to New York which my father had been commissioned to buy for Mr. Lenox. There used to be a story, which I daresay you have heard, of how Turner was one day showing some great man or other round his gallery, and Turner's father looked in through a half-open door and said, in a low voice, 'That 'ere's done,' and that Turner taking no *apparent* notice, but continuing to attend his visitor, the old man's head appeared again, after an interval of five or six minutes, and said, in a louder tone, 'That 'ere will be spiled.' I think Landseer used to tell this story as having happened when he and one of his many noble friends were going the round of Turner's gallery about the time that Turner's chop or steak was being cooked.

"6, MOIRA PLACE, SOUTHAMPTON,
"*June 30th*, 1884.

"MY DEAR MR. RUSKIN,

"After sending you that photograph of the *Téméraire*, it occurred to me to see if I could find out anything about the ship or her building in an old book I have (Charnock's 'Marine Architecture'), and I was surprised to find there, in a list of ships in our navy between the years 1700 and 1800, TWO ships of that name—one a seventy-four, taken from the French in 1759, the other a ninety-eight gun ship, built at Chatham in 1798. This made me look again at Mr. Thornbury's account of the ship and her title, and leads me to doubt three things he has stated: first, that the ship (if she was the French *Téméraire*) 'had no history in our navy before Trafalgar;' secondly, that 'she was taken at the battle of the Nile;' and, thirdly, that the *Téméraire* which fought at Trafalgar was French at all.

"The model we have here, and which has the name *Téméraire* carved upon her stern, is a ninety-eight gun ship, and would be the one built at Chatham in 1798. But what I am driving at, and *the point* to which all this confusion leads, is, that after all, perhaps, dear old Turner was perfectly right in his first title for his picture of 'The Fighting *Téméraire*,' for if she was the old seventy-four gun ship (and in the engraving she looks like a two-decker) that he saw being towed to the shipbreaker's yard, she, having been in our navy for years, may have been distinguished among sailors from the other and newer *Téméraire* by that name; while it is significant (*if true*) that Turner, when he reluctantly gave up his title, said, 'Well, then, call her the *Old Téméraire*.'

"Thornbury's book, which I have not seen since it was published until I borrowed it a few days back, appears to me a sort of hashed-up life of Brown, Jones, and Robinson, with badly done bits of Turner floating about in it. I have copied the passage from it referring to the *Téméraire* upon a separate sheet, also the history of the capture of the *French Téméraire* from the *Gentleman's Magazine*.

" I have only now to add, in answer to your last and kindest of notes, that I read French in a bumbly sort of way, like a French yoke of oxen dragging a load of stone uphill upon a cross road, but that my wife reads it easily. Twice, dear Mr. Ruskin, you have said, ' Is it not strange you should have sent me something about Turner just as I was employing a French critic to write his life ? ' Now, I believe that nothing is really strange between those where on the one side there is perfect truth and honesty of purpose, and on the other faith in, and love and reverence for, that purpose.

" Forgive me if I have said too much; and believe me, yours faithfully and affectionately,

"ROBT. C. LESLIE."

EXTRACT FROM A LIST OF SHIPS IN OUR NAVY BETWEEN THE YEARS 1700 AND 1800.

" *Téméraire*, 1,685 tons, 74 guns, taken from the French, 1759.
" *Téméraire*, 2,121 tons, 98 guns, *built* at *Chatham*, 1798."

Charnock's "Marine Architecture" (1802).

" Saturday, Sept. 15th, 1759, Admiral Boscawen arrived at Spithead with His Majestie's ships *Namur*, etc., and the *Modeste* and *Téméraire*, prizes. The *Téméraire* is a fine seventy-four-gun ship, forty-two-pounders below, eight fine brass guns abaft her mainmast, ten brass guns on her quarter, very little hurt."

Gentleman's Magazine, September, 1759.

HOW THE OLD *TÉMÉRAIRE* WAS TAKEN.

Extract of a letter from Admiral Boscawen to Mr. Cleveland, Secretary of the Admiralty, dated off Cape St. Vincent, August 20th, 1759:——

" I acquainted you in my last of my return to Gibraltar to refit. As soon as the ships were near ready, I ordered the *Lyme* and *Gibraltar* frigates, the first to cruise off Malaga, and the last from Estepona to Ceuta Point, to look out, and give me timely notice of the enemy's approach. On the 17th, at 8 p.m., the *Gibraltar* made the signal of their appearance, fourteen sail, on the Barbary shore. . . . I got under sail as fast as possible, and was out of the bay before 10 p.m., with fourteen sail of the line. At daylight I saw the *Gibraltar*, and soon after seven sail of large ships lying to; but on our not answering their signals they made sail from us. We had a fresh gale, and came up with them fast till

about noon, when it fell little wind.
About half an hour past two some of
the headmost ships began to engage, but
I could not get up to the *Ocean* till near
four. In about half an hour my ship
the *Namur's* mizen-mast and both topsail-
yards were shot away; the enemy then
made all the sail they could. I shifted
my flag to the *Newark*, and soon after
the *Centaur*, of seventy-four guns, struck.

" I pursued all night, and in the morning of the 19th saw only four sail of the
line standing in for the land. . . . We
were not above three miles from them,
and not above five leagues from the shore,
but very little wind. About nine the
Ocean ran amongst the breakers, and the
three others anchored. I sent the *Intrepid*
and *America* to destroy the *Ocean*. Capt.
Pratten, having anchored, could not get
in ; but Capt. Kirk performed that service
alone. On his first firing at the *Ocean* she
struck. Capt. Kirk sent his officers on

board. M. de la Clue, having one leg broke, and the other wounded, had been landed about half an hour ; but they found the captain, M. La Comte, De Carne, and several officers and men on board ; Capt. Kirk, after taking them out, finding it impossible to bring the ship off, set her on fire. Capt. Bentley, of the *Warspite*, was ordered against the *Téméraire*, of seventy-four guns, and brought her off with little damage, the officers and men all on board. At the same time, Vice-Admiral Broderick, with his division, burnt the *Redoutable*, her officers and men having quitted her, being bulged ; and brought the *Modest*, of sixty-four guns, off very little damaged. I have the pleasure to acquaint their Lordships, that most of His Majestie's ships under my command sailed better than those of the enemy." . . .

From the *Gentleman's Magazine* for September, 1759.

" I could not resist copying this letter in full.—R. L."

"I have just read the appendix to your 'Art of England,' and was particularly interested in the account of how you felt that cold south-west wind up in Lancashire. This is the second, if not third season, that we have remarked them here in the south of England, though I think the south-westers of this spring were more bitter than usual. I told you, I believe, that my wife and I started away for Spain this April. Now, on all this journey, down the west coast of France, across the north of Spain, to Barcelona, in lat. 41°, and up through Central France again, I watched and noted day by day the same strange sky that we have with us, the same white sun, with that opaque sheet about him, or else covered by dark dull vapours, from which now and then something fell in unexpected drops, followed by still more unexpected clearing-ups. There were one or two days of intense sunshine, followed always by bad pale sunsets, and often

accompanied by driving storms of wind
and dust. But, returning to the cold
south-westers, I don't suppose you care
much for the why of them, even if I am
right, which is, that I think we owe them
to the very great and early break-up for
the last year or two of the northern ice,*
which in the western ocean was met with
before March this year, several steamers
being in collision with it, while one report
from Newfoundland spoke of an iceberg
aground there I am afraid to say how
many miles long and over a hundred feet
high. Now, when I was young (I am
fifty-eight), and a good deal upon that sea,
it was always thought that there was no
chance of falling in with ice earlier than
quite the *end* of May, and this was excep-
tional, the months of July and August
being the iceberg months. (I have seen

* Yes ; but what makes the ice break up?
I think the plague-wind blows every way, every-
where, all round the world.—J. R.

a large one off the Banks in September.)
This early arrival of the northern ice
seems to show that the mild winters
have extended up even into the Arctic
Circle, and points to some real increase
in the power or heat of the sun.*

"I have many things I should like to
talk over with you, but fear that will
never be, unless you are able to come
some time and have a few days' rest and
boating with me."

* I don't believe it a bit. I think the sun's
going out.—J. R.

CORRESPONDENCE, DIARY NOTES, AND

EXTRACTS FROM BOOKS,

ILLUSTRATING

PRÆTERITA.

ARRANGED BY

JOHN RUSKIN, LL.D.,

HONORARY STUDENT OF CHRIST CHURCH
AND HONORARY FELLOW OF CORPUS CHRISTI COLLEGE, OXFORD.

PART II.

GEORGE ALLEN,
SUNNYSIDE, ORPINGTON, KENT
1887.

Price One Shilling.

DILECTA.

CORRESPONDENCE, DIARY NOTES, AND

EXTRACTS FROM BOOKS,

.

ILLUSTRATING

PRÆTERITA.

ARRANGED BY

JOHN RUSKIN, LL.D.,

HONORARY STUDENT OF CHRIST CHURCH,
AND HONORARY FELLOW OF CORPUS CHRISTI COLLEGE, OXFORD.

PART II.

GEORGE ALLEN,
SUNNYSIDE, ORPINGTON, KENT.
1887.

Printed by Hazell, Watson, & Viney, Ld., London and Aylesbury.

DILECTA.

PART II.

Mr. Leslie's notes on the *Téméraire* and her double have led to some farther correspondence respecting both this ship and Nelson's own, which must still take precedence of any connected with the early numbers of 'Præterita.'

"DEAREST MR. RUSKIN,

"Mr. W. Hale White, of the Admiralty, has, as you will see, written to me about the *Téméraires*, and I thought you ought to know what he has to say on the subject, especially that postscript to his note about placing some short history of the ship under

Turner's picture. Also the fact of the old French ship being *sold* in the year 1784, when there could have been no tugs on the river, and when Turner was only nine years old, seems to settle the point as to which of the two ships it was, in favour of ' the English *Téméraire.*' Still, as boyish impressions in a mind like Turner's must have been *very strong*, it is just possible that he may have seen the last of both ships when knocking about the Thames below London.

" In the *picture*, as I said before, the ship is a *two*-decker, and her having her spars and sails bent to the yards looks very like a time before steam, when a hulk without some kind of jury-rig would be almost useless, even to a ship-breaker, if he had to *move her* at all.

" Ever affectionately,

" ROBT. C. LESLIE."

" ADMIRALTY, WHITEHALL, S.W.,
" 20th November, 1886.

" DEAR SIR,

" I see in Mr. Ruskin's ' Dilecta ' a letter of yours about the *Téméraire*. Perhaps you will like to know the facts about the two vessels you name.

" The *Téméraire* taken by Admiral Boscawen from the French in 1759 was sold in June 1784.

" The *Téméraire* which Turner saw was consequently the second *Téméraire*. She was fitted for a prison ship at Plymouth in 1812. In 1819 she became a receiving ship, and was sent to Sheerness. There she remained till she was sold in 1838.

" What Mr. Thornbury means by ' the grand old vessel that had been taken prisoner at the Nile ' I do not know. I may add that it cannot be ascertained now, at any rate without prolonged search amongst documents in the Record Office, whether the second *Téméraire* was sold ' all standing,' that is to say, with masts and yards as painted ; but it is very improbable, as she had been a receiving ship, that her masts and yards were in her when she left the service.

"Truly yours,

"W. HALE WHITE.

" R. C. Leslie, Esq.

" It seems to me a pity, considering the importance of the picture, that the truth about the subject of it should not somewhere be easily accessible to everybody who cares to know it — say upon the picture-frame. I would undertake to put down in tabular form the principal points in the vessel's biography, if it were thought worth while."

I should at all events be most grateful if Mr. Hale White would furnish me with such abstract, as, whether used in the National Gallery or not, many people would like to have it put beneath the engraving.

In a subsequent note from Mr. Leslie about the pike fishing at Lord Egremont's, he gives me this little sketch of the way Turner rigged his ship for him with leaves torn out of his sketch book.

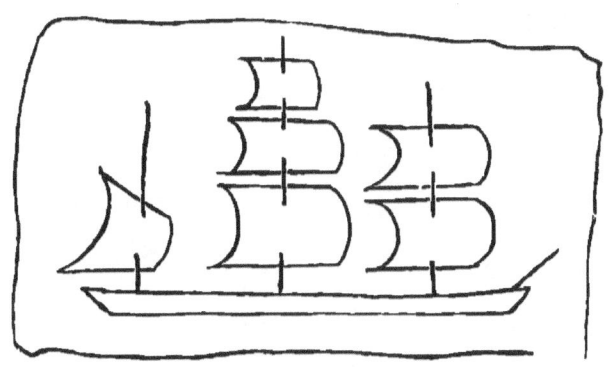

The following note, also from Mr. Leslie, with its cutting from *St. James's Gazette*; and the next one, for which I am extremely grateful, on the words 'dickey' and 'deck,' bear further on Turner's meaning in the little black steamer which guides the funeral march of the line of battle ship,—and foretell the

time now come when ships have neither
masts, sails, nor decks, but are driven under
water with their crews under hatches.

" DEAREST MR. RUSKIN,

" I have just finished 'The State of
Denmark,' which is delightful, especially
the story of the row of expectant little
pigs. They are wonderful animals—our
English elephant I think as to mental
capacity. But they always have an interest to me above other edible live stock,
in the way they make the best of life
on shipboard; and when you can spare
time to look at the enclosed little paper
of mine, you will find that others have
found their society cheerful.

" I have been reading all the old sea
voyages I can get hold of lately, with a
view to learn all I can about the way they
handled their canvas in the days of sails
(for my 'Sea-Wings'), and I come con-
stantly across the pig on board ship in

such books. For some reason or other,
sailors don't care to have parsons on
board ship. This perhaps dates back to
time of Jonah; and your passages in this
'Præterita,' in which you describe and
dispose of the teaching of some modern
ones, are quite perfect, and in your
'making short work' best style.

"Ever yours affectionately,

"ROBT. C. LESLIE."

"In smaller vessels, carrying no passengers,
pigs and goats were seldom home-fed; but
were turned loose to cater for themselves
among the odds and ends in the waist or
deck between the poop and forecastle.
Some of the poultry, too, soon became
tame enough to be allowed the run of this
part of a ship; the ducks and geese finding a particular pleasure in paddling in the
wash about the lee scuppers. Pigs have
always proved a thriving stock on a ship-
farm, and the one that pays the best.

Some old skippers assert, indeed, that, like Madeira, pig is improved greatly by a voyage to India and back round the Cape; and that none but those who have tasted boiled leg of pork on board a homeward bound Indiaman know much about the matter. But here also, as in so many other things, there was a drawback. Pigs are such cheerful creatures at sea that, as an old soft-hearted seaman once remarked, you get too partial towards them, and feel after dinner sometimes as though you had eaten an old messmate. Next to the pig the goat was the most useful stock on a sea-farm. This animal soon makes itself at home on shipboard; it has good sea-legs, and is blessed with an appetite that nothing in the shape of vegetable fibre comes amiss to, from an armful of shavings from the carpenter's berth to an old newspaper. Preserved milk was, of course, unknown in those times, and the officers of a large pas-

senger-ship would rather have gone to
sea without a doctor (to say nothing of
a parson) than without a cow or some
nanny-goats. Even on board a man-of-
war the admiral or captain generally had
at least one goat for his own use, while
space was found for live stock for other
ward-room officers. But model-farming
and home-feeding was the rule then as
now in a King's ship; and it is related
that, on board one of these vessels, the
first lieutenant ordered the ship's painter
to give the feet and bills of the admiral's
geese that were stowed in coops upon the
quarter-deck a coat of black once a week,
so that the nautical eye might not be
offended by any intrusion of colour not
allowed in the service.

"The general absence of colour among
real sea-fowl is very marked; and when,
as it sometimes happened, a gay rooster
escaped overboard after an exciting chase
round the decks with Jemmy Ducks, and

fluttered helplessly down upon the bosom of the sea, his glowing plumage looked strangely out of harmony with things as he sat drifting away upon the waste of waters."

" BERKELEY, GLOUCESTERSHIRE,
" *Oct.* 29*th*, 1886.

" MY DEAR SIR,

" I notice in the first chapter of ' Præterita ' that you profess yourself unable to find out the derivation of the word ' dickey ' as applied to the rumble of a carriage.

" At the risk of being the hundredth or so who has volunteered the information, I send you an extract from Dr. Brewer's ' Dictionary of Phrase and Fable ' :—

" ' Dickey. — The rumble behind a carriage ; also a leather apron, a child's bib, and a false shirt or front. Dutch *dekken*, Germ. *decken*, Sax. *thecan*, Lat. *tego*, to cover.'

" I suppose that the word ' deck ' has its derivation from the same source.

" Sincerely hoping that you may be speedily restored to health,

" I am, dear Sir,

" Yours very faithfully,

" HERBERT E. COOKE."

The following extract from a letter written to his sister by a young surgeon on board the *Victory*, gives more interesting lights on Nelson's character than I caught from all Southey's Life of him :—

" On my coming on board I found that the recommendation which my former services in the Navy had procured for me from several friends, had conciliated towards me the good opinion of his lordship and his officers, and I immediately became one of the family. It may amuse you, my dear sister, to read the brief journal of a day such as we here pass it at sea in this

fine climate and in these smooth seas, on
board one of the largest ships in the
Navy, as she mounts 110 guns, one of
which, carrying a 24lb. shot, occupies a
very distinguished station in my apartment.

" Jan. 12.—Off the Straits of Bonifacio,
a narrow arm of the sea between Corsica
and Sardinia.—We have been baffled in our
progress towards the rendezvous of the
squadron at the Madeline Islands for some
days past by variable and contrary winds,
but we expect to arrive at our destination
to-night or to-morrow morning. To re-
sume, my dear sister, the journal of a day.
At 6 o'clock my servant brings a light and
informs me of the hour, wind, weather,
and course of the ship, when I immediately
dress and generally repair to the deck, the
dawn of day at this season and latitude
being apparent at about half or three-
quarters of an hour past six. Breakfast
is announced in the Admiral's cabin, where
Lord Nelson,—Rear-Admiral Murray, the

Captain of the Fleet,---Captain Hardy, Commander of the *Victory*, the chaplain, secretary, one or two officers of the ship, and your humble servant, assemble and breakfast on tea, hot rolls, toast, cold tongue, etc., which when finished we repair upon deck to enjoy the majestic sight of the rising sun (scarcely ever obscured by clouds in this fine climate) surmounting the smooth and placid waves of the Mediterranean which supports the lofty and tremendous bulwarks of Britain, following in regular train their Admiral in the *Victory*. Between the hours of seven and two there is plenty of time for business, study, writing, and exercise, which different occupations, together with that of occasionally visiting the hospital of the ship when required by the surgeon, I endeavour to vary in such a manner as to afford me sufficient employment. At two o'clock a band of music plays till within a quarter of three, when the drum beats the tune

called 'The Roast Beef of Old England' to announce the Admiral's dinner,
which is served up exactly at three o'clock,
and which generally consists of three
courses and a dessert of the choicest fruit,
together with three or four of the best
wines, champagne and claret not excepted;
and—what exceeds the relish of the best
viands and most exquisite wines,—if a
person does not feel himself perfectly at
his ease it must be his own fault, such is
the urbanity and hospitality which reign
here, notwithstanding the numerous titles,
the four orders of knighthood, worn by
Lord Nelson, and the well-earned laurels
which he has acquired. Coffee and
liqueurs close the dinner about half-past
four or five o'clock, after which the company generally walk the deck, where the
band of music plays for near an hour. At
six o'clock tea is announced, when the
company again assemble in the Admiral's
cabin, where tea is served up before seven

o'clock, and, as we are inclined, the party continue to converse with his lordship, who at this time generally unbends himself, though he is at all times as free from stiffness and pomp as a regard to proper dignity will admit, and is very communicative. At eight o'clock a rummer of punch with cake or biscuit is served up, soon after which we wish the Admiral a good night (who is generally in bed before nine o'clock). For my own part, not having been accustomed to go to bed quite so early, I generally read an hour, or spend one with the officers of the ship, several of whom are old acquaintances, or to whom I have been known by character. Such, my dear sister, is the journal of a day at sea in fine or at least moderate weather, in which this floating castle goes through the water with the greatest imaginable steadiness, and I have not yet been long enough on board to experience bad weather."

I must find room for a word or two
more of Mr. Leslie's, for the old floating
castles as against steam; and then pass to
matters more personal to me.

"MOIRA PLACE, *Sept.* 20*th*, 1886.

"I believe that the whole of the
present depression in what is called trade
is entirely due to the exaggerated estimate
of the economy of steam, especially when
applied to the production of real wealth
upon the land; also to the idea that
the wealth of the world is in any way
increased by making a lawn tennis court
of it, the world, and knocking goods to
and fro as fast as possible across it by
steam. No doubt I shall be told that I
am quite out of my depth in this matter,
and that France (a really self-supporting
country) is at least five hundred years
behind the times. I won't apologize
for sending you enclosed, which, for the
animal's sake alone, I fear is true. The
cutting is from the *Times* of the 18th:—

"A writer in the *Revue Scientifique* affirms that, from a comparison of animal and steam power, the former is the cheaper power in France, whatever may be the case in other countries. In the conversion of chemical to mechanical energy, 90 per cent. is lost in the machine, against 68 in the animal. M. Sanson, the writer above referred to, finds that the steam horse-power, contrary to what is generally believed, is often materially exceeded by the horse. The cost of traction on the Mount Parnasse-Bastille line of railway he found to be for each car, daily, 57 f., while the same work done by the horse cost only 47 f.; and he believes that for moderate powers the conversion of chemical into mechanical energy is more economically effected through animals than through steam engines."

The following two letters from Turner to Mr. W. E. Cooke, which I find among various papers relating to his work given to me at various times, are of great interest in showing the number of points Turner used to take into consideration before determining on anything, and his strict sense of duty and courtesy. The blank line, of which we are left to conjecture the meaning, is much longer in the real letter :—

"Wednesday morning.

" DEAR SIR,

"I have taken the earliest opportunity to return you the touched proof and corrected St. Michael Mounts. I lament that your brother could not forward the Poole, or Mr. Bulmer the proof sheets, for if the two cannot be sent so as to arrive here before *Tuesday next,* I shall be upon the wing for London again, where I hope to be in about a fortnight from this time ; therefore, you'll judge how practicable you can make the sending the parcel in time, or waiting until I get to Queen Ann

Street, N.W. Your number coming out on the 10th of December I think impossible; but to this I offer only an opinion (what difference would it make if the two numbers of the Coast, Daniel's and yours, came out on the same day?). All I can say, I'll not hinder you, if I can avoid it, one moment. Therefore employ Mr. Pye if you think proper, but, as you know, there should be some objection on my part as to co - operation with him without - - — - ; yet to forego the assistance of his abilities for any feeling of mine is by no means proper to the majority of subscribers to the work.

"Yours most truly,

"J. M. W. TURNER.

" P.S.—I am not surprised at Mr. Ellis writing such a note about his signature. Be so good as put the enclosed into the Twopenny Post Box. The book which I now send be kind enough to keep for me until I return, and expect it to be useful in the descriptions of Cornwall."

"*Thursday E^g Decr 16, 1813.*

" DEAR SIR,

"From your letter of this morning I expected the pleasure of seeing you, but being disappointed, I feel the necessity of requesting you will, under the peculiar case in which the MSS. of St. Michael and Poole are placed, desire Mr. Coombe to deviate wholly from them ; and if he has introduced anything which seems to approximate, to be so good as to remove the same, as any likeness in the descriptions (though highly complimentary to my endeavours) must compel me to claim them—by an immediate appeal as to their originality. Moreover, as I now shall not charge or will receive any remuneration whatever for them, they are consequently at my disposal, and ultimately subject only to my use—in vindication; never do I hope they will be called upon to appear, but if ever offer'd that they will be looked upon with liberality and candour, and not considered in any way detrimental to the interests of the Proprietors of the Southern Coast work.

"Have the goodness to return the corrected proof of St. Michael, which I sent from Yorkshire with the MS. of Poole; and desire Mr. Bulmer either to send me all the proof sheets, or in your seeing them destroyed you will much oblige

"Yours most truly,

"J. M. W. TURNER."

I find in my father's diary of the journey of 1833 some notes on the state of Basle city and its environs at the time of our passing through them, which are extremely interesting to me in their cool-ness, especially in connection with the general caution which influenced my father in all other kinds of danger. No man could be more prudent in guarding against ordinary chances of harm, and in what may be shortly expressed as looking to the girths of life. But here he is travelling with his wife and son through a district in dispute between not only military forces but political factions, without appearing for an instant to have contemplated changing his route, or felt the slightest uneasiness in passing through the area of most active warfare. My mother seems to have been exactly of the same mind, —which is more curious still, for indeed I never once saw the expression of fear on my father's face, through all his life, at anything; but my mother was easily frightened if postillions drove too fast, or the carriage leaned threateningly aside; while here she passes through the midst of bands of angry and armed villagers without a word of objection.

" Baden (Swiss Baden, 5th August, 1833).—We heard here of the Basle people fighting with peasantry and burning their villages; and of a battle betwixt Liechstal and Basle soldiers on Saturday; the latter were driven into the town; 80 killed and 400 prisoners. We came to Stein to dine; a single house on the borders of the Rhine, commanding a beautiful view of that river and plains beyond it, and Black Forest in the distance. We had eighteen miles to go to Basle, but, hearing Swiss gates were shut, we crossed into Baden state at Rheinfeld, where there are some very old buildings and two wooden bridges; the river rolls like a troubled sea. Coming towards Basle we saw soldiers with several large brass cannon, in a field which the peasants were ploughing, on an eminence commanding the road. We arrived at 7 o'clock at Three Kings, Basle, and early next morning I walked to cathedral;

found many of the first houses with windows entirely closed, in mourning for officers lost in battle of Saturday; and a report prevailed of there being a plot to admit the peasantry into the town to fire it in the night. The people were much alarmed.

"Tuesday, 6th August, we left by a gate just opened to let us pass, being sent from another gate we tried, and which we saw, after we got out, had its drawbridge entirely cut away. The guns were placed with twigs and basketwork in embrasures, soldiers stood on the walls ready, and looking out over the country with glasses. The road lay through Liechstal, where the strife was. It is a fine road, as the best in England, generally much frequented, and the country is beautiful and rich in cultivation; but on twenty-seven miles of this fine road we met neither carriage, diligence, gig, nor waggon. The land seemed deserted, only a peasant occasionally in the fields. We soon met a small band of armed peasants in the act of stopping a small market-cart which had preceded us. The man, when released, went quickly off. They let us pass. We then met two bands of armed peasants, very Irish-like in costume, and having guns swung behind or in their hands, about fifteen or twenty in each body,— part, we suppose, of the Liberals who had defeated the Tories of Basle.* They looked, and lifted their hats, and said nothing to us. Approaching Liechstal, we met a Swiss car with eight or ten gentlemen in plain clothes, well armed; also cars filled with armed peasants, and a few soldiers at their side. We entered Liechstal, and found every street barri-

* Papa cannot bring himself to think of anybody in Irish-like costume as Conservative. It was Basle that was liberally and Protestantially endeavouring to make the men of Liechstal abjure their Catholic errors.

caded breast high with pine logs, except
at entrance, where an opening was left
just wide enough for cart or carriage, and
a gate at the other end. These gentlemen, I was afterwards told, were Polish
refugees, who served the artillery of the
peasantry against the Basle people, who
had refused to shelter them, whilst the
Liechstal people had received them kindly."

And so all notice of states of siege,
whether at Liechstal or anywhere else,
ends in my father's diary; and he con-
tinues in perfect tranquillity to give account
of his notes on the roads, inns, and agriculture of Switzerland.

Of which, however, the reader will, I
think, have pleasure in seeing sóme further passages, representing, not through
any gilded mists of memory, but with
mercantile precision of entering day by
day, the aspect of Switzerland at the time
when we first saw it, half a century ago.

" 18th July. We left Berne early, and
went eighteen miles to Thun. The road
is one of the best possible, beginning
through an avenue of trees, large and
fine, and proceeding to Thun through
fields of amazing beauty, bordered with
fruit trees; the corn sometimes bordering
the road without enclosure. The cottages,
houses, farms, inns, all the way, each and
all remarkable for neatness, largeness, and
beauty. We left our carriage at the
Freyenhof Inn, and took boat, three
hours' rowing, to Neuhaus, then one league
in char-à-banc ; through Unterseen to
Interlachen, a sweet watering-place sort
of a village, with one hotel and many
very elegant boarding-houses, where per-
sons stop to take excursions to neigh-
bouring hills. We took boat down lake
Brienz as far as waterfall of Giesbach,
the finest fall next to those of Rhine I
have yet seen; but the best thing was
the Swiss family in the small inn up the

hill opposite to the fall. The old man, his son, and two daughters, sung Swiss songs in the sweetest and most affecting manner, infinitely finer than opera singing, because true alike to Nature and to music; * no grimace nor affectation, nor strained efforts to produce effect. The tunes were well chosen, and the whole very delightful; more so than any singing I remember. We returned to Interlachen, where the Justice condemned Salvador to pay twelve francs for a carriage not used, which he had hired to go to the Staubbach. Next morning we returned by water to Thun to breakfast, and again to Berne, where we had very nice rooms, with fine prospect.

"The portico walks in almost every street in Berne are very convenient for

* I shall make this sentence the text of what I have to say, when I have made a few more experiments in our schools here, of the use of music in peasant education.

rain or sun: it is in this like Chester,
though the one appearing a very new
town, and the other very old. We left
Berne 22nd July by a narrow but not
bad road through Summiswald; dined at
Hutwyl; slept at Sursee, in the Catholic
canton of Lucerne. The hill and dale
country we passed through to the very
end of the Berne canton was a scene of
unequalled loveliness out of this canton.
The face of the country was varied, but
the richness of cultivation the same, and
the houses so large, and yet so neat and
comfortable. This is, indeed, a country for
which a man might sigh, and almost die,
of regret, to be exiled from. I have seen
nothing at all approaching to it in the
neatest parts of England. The town of
Berne is equally remarkable for good
though not lofty buildings, and for clean-
liness and neatness. The street-sweepers
were women; and I never saw a city or
town so beautifully kept. I walked up

many back streets and lanes, all in the most perfect order; and the country seen from the cathedral terrace and ramparts is just suited to such a town. There is no formed, squared, or trimmed neatness, but every field, and hedge, and tree, and garden, seem to be tended and kept in the finest state possible. The variety of scenery on the grandest scale,—the snowy Alps, the lower Alps, the woods on undulating grounds, or sloping down from the mountain tops; the fine river passing round the town; the rich cornfields, meadows, and fruit trees, abounding over all; nature doing so much, and man just bestowing the care and culture required, and applying art only where it seems to improve nature.

"If any country on earth can be deemed perfect as far as nature and art can make it, the canton of Berne is that country. The farm houses are each a picture, and the peasantry are as beautiful and healthy

as the country. They express contentment.
Their costume is handsome, excepting the
black, stiff, whalebone-lace ears of immense
size from the women's heads; when they
wear black lace over their heads partially,
the rest of their dress is extremely be-
coming. On Wednesday, July 17th, we
rode to Hofwyl Farm, Mr. Fellenberg's
Institution, combining a large fine boarding-
house for eighty to ninety young gentlemen
of fortune, where all branches of education
are taught, and agriculture added if they
choose; and a school for poor boys and
girls, and for masters of country schools
to learn.

"Some Russian princes have attended
the boarding school. The expense, about
three thousand francs yearly. Everything is
made on the farm—bread, butter, clothes,
shoes, etc. There are from two hundred
and eighty to three hundred acres of land
in cultivation, lying in a sort of basin
sloping gently away from house towards

a piece of water. It is impossible to con-
ceive anything so beautiful for a farm as
this. There being four hundred people
about it there is no want of labour; and
added to the usual Swiss neatness, there
is the completeness of an amateur farmer
possessing ample means. There were
fifty-four milk cows kept on hay and
potatoes under cover. (The want of cattle
in the field is always a drawback to a
foreign landscape.) The oxen very handsome. The system of farming same as
Scotch, only one new product seen by a
Scotch amateur whom we met. Italian
rye grass, very fine. The poorer young
men cutting hay, all very happy. The
workshops, the washing-houses, the out-
houses all very perfect, but in implements
or machinery nothing new. It was the
beauty of the situation on a fine day, and
the fulness and apparent comfort, that
struck the observer particularly."